# Spooky Cutie
## Halloween Coloring Book

**Published by Color Whimsy**

Eerie and delightful. Step into a whimsical world where spooky meets cute—adorable ghosts, playful pumpkins, and cheerful bats are just waiting for your splash of color. Join in the fun, and bring these quirky, haunted-yet-happy characters to life!

## HOW TO USE THIS BOOK

We've selected standard quality paper to keep this book affordable, given the paper options available on Amazon. This paper works very well with colored pencils and alcohol-based markers. To avoid any ink bleed-through when using pens or markers, we recommend placing a blank sheet of paper behind the page that you're coloring.

We appreciate your understanding and look forward to seeing what you create!

Made in the USA
Las Vegas, NV
10 September 2024

95106621R00072